AWESOME HITOPADESH Tales

6-in-1 Series
Awesome Hitopadesh Tales

ISBN: 978-93-5049-414-1

Printed in 2018

© Shree Book Centre

Retold by
Sunita Pant Bansal

Published by

Shree Book Centre

8, Kakad Industrial Estate, S. Keer Marg, off L. J. Road
Matunga (west), Mumbai 400 016, India
Tel: +91-22-2437 7516 / 2437 4559 / 2438 0907
Fax: +91-22-2430 9183
Email: sales@shreebookcentre.com
Website: **www.shreebookcentre.com**

Contents

Preface

Hitopadesh has been coined from two words—*Hita* meaning "welfare or benefit" and *Updesh* meaning "advice or counsel". Originally written in Sanskrit by Narayana Pandit, around AD 1675, the Hitopadesh stories are considered similar to the Panchatantra tales. The stories help young minds learn the philosophy of life and grow into responsible adults.

Like the Panchantantra, the Hitopadesh tales too feature animal characters. Some of them are written in a story-within-a-story format. These stories have travelled to several parts of the world, capturing the imagination of children and helping them learn good habits and values.

This volume contains six carefully-picked moral stories with colourful illustrations. Written in simple language, the stories are easy for children to read and understand. The speech bubbles in the story will help children understand what the characters think and feel. The meanings of difficult words, at the end of the book, will enrich children's vocabulary.

The Curious Monkey

Once upon a time, there lived a lion and a lioness with their three little cubs. The cubs were very naughty and always up to some mischief or the other. They would often run away and hide from their mother or climb up a tree and get hurt. Sometimes, they stumbled and fell into a well.

The cubs' mother had a difficult time getting them out of the mess they were in. But she never scolded them or complained about them to their father. She always thought, "They are just being curious."

One day, the lion was at home and saw how naughty his cubs were. So, he told them, "If you promise not to run around and trouble your mother the whole day, I will tell you an interesting story at night."

The cubs were eager to hear the story. So, they behaved themselves the whole day.

As promised, the lion called the cubs at night and started telling them the story.

* * *

Once, there lived a troop of monkeys. The curious monkeys were always running up and down the trees and here and there, searching and exploring. One day, they reached a place where a temple was being built. A rich merchant had employed a few men to construct the temple.

The monkeys started watching the masons and carpenters at work. They came there every morning and observed the men from the treetop. They also played around the construction site, but they never went close to it or touched anything.

Now, there was a very naughty baby monkey among them. He was curious about everything.

The baby monkey touched everything and looked at them closely.

The mother monkey warned him to stay away from trouble, but he never listened to her and got into trouble often. He would entangle himself in a tree branch or get hurt while looking at a sharp object.

When the monkeys started playing near the construction site, the baby monkey was very happy, as there were so many things to look at, touch and pick up.

One day, while the mother monkey was fast asleep, the baby monkey went very close to the construction site.

He started looking curiously at the tools and other things lying around.

Now, a carpenter had split a beam into two halves and had inserted a wedge in between. As it was a hot day, he had taken a break to rest for some time. Seeing no one around, the baby monkey started poking the beams.

He tried to separate them. When he could not move the beams, he started pulling the wedge between the beams.

He pulled it so hard that the wedge came out. The poor monkey was trapped in between the two beams. Before anyone could help him, he was crushed to death.

Thus, his curiosity cost him his life, leaving his friends and family very sad.

* * *

The lion concluded his story by saying, "You see, my children, if you are very naughty, you will get into trouble and also create trouble for others. You should listen to your mother and not trouble her so much."

From then on, the cubs listened to their mother and acted in a responsible manner. The lioness was very happy and taught her cubs the right way to behave.

Moral: Do not be too naughty. It can lead to trouble.

The Birds and the Monkeys

Once, there was a swan who wished to explore new places. So, one fine day, he bid farewell to his family and flew away. Soon he reached a river. There he saw a frog who had hurt his foot and was crying in pain.

The swan felt sorry for the frog. He thought, "I must advise the frog not to jump on the rocks but swim in the water until his foot heals."

When he saw the swan, the frog got scared and jumped. Unfortunately, he could not jump high enough because of his injured foot. He hit a rock hard and died instantly.

The swan was very sad seeing this. A crane, who was sitting nearby, had seen the entire incident. He went to the swan and said, "Do not waste your time advising fools. Haven't you heard the story of the birds and the monkeys?" The curious swan replied, "No, I have not. Please tell me the story."

So, the crane began to narrate the story.

* * *

Once, there was a lush, green salmali tree on the banks of the Narmada river. The tree had many branches in which many birds lived.

One day, a family of birds flying that way came across the tree. They immediately liked it and decided to make it their home.

They chose a secure branch and started building a nest on it. They worked hard and built a big and cosy nest. Soon, the mother bird laid a few eggs in the nest. She told her elder children, "Little ones! Make sure the eggs do not crack before time. Your younger brothers and sisters are in them."

One day, the father bird said, "The rains are going to start soon and the eggs will hatch. Mother bird, you take care of the eggs. The rest of us will collect all the food that we can get. We need to store some food for the rainy season."

Close to the salmali tree lived a troop of monkeys. They were always busy playing. They did not bother to make a house for themselves or collect food for the rainy season.

Finally, the rains came. The birds were safe and dry in their nest.

But the monkeys were huddled together
under the tree, wet and shivering.

The birds saw the monkeys from their nest
and felt sorry for them. They decided to advise
the monkeys.

The birds said, "Why did you waste your time playing? You have hands and feet. You could have easily used them to make a home for yourself. But you chose not to use them and now you have to suffer."

This really upset the monkeys. They said, "Are you teasing us?"

The birds said, "No, of course not! We are just trying to tell you that we don't have hands. We have to use our beaks and work hard to make our house and collect food. We plan ahead for the future. You too should prepare like us."

This angered the monkeys. They decided to teach the birds a lesson.

When it stopped raining, the monkeys ran up the tree, broke the birds' nest and smashed their eggs.

The birds kept pleading with them, but the monkeys refused to listen.

* * *

The crane ended the story saying, "So you see, there is no point giving advice to fools."

The crane then explained what he meant, "The advice is always misunderstood and it leads to trouble, just like it did for the birds."

The swan realized his mistake and decided not to give advice to others, unless asked. He flew away from the river and continued his journey.

Moral: Do not give unwanted advice.

The Donkey in a Lion's Skin

Once upon a time, there lived a poor washerman in a city. He worked very hard to earn his living. The washerman woke up at dawn and went to many houses to collect dirty clothes. Then he carried the heavy pile of dirty clothes to a pond near his house to wash them.

After washing the clothes, he dried them in the open area around the pond.

Once the clothes were dry, he ironed and folded them and returned them to the respective houses. All this work tired him completely.

The washerman longed to take a nap in the afternoon. He often said to himself, "I wish I had some help." However, there was no one to help him.

One day, as he was walking to the pond, the washerman found a lion's skin on the ground. He picked it up and kept it carefully in his house.

The next day, the washerman saw a donkey wandering in the fields. He thought, "I don't think this donkey belongs to anyone. I will take him with me and use him to help me with my work."

From the next day onwards, the washerman made the donkey carry the heavy load of clothes.

Thus, he was less tired and able to wash more clothes. His business prospered.

The washerman began to earn a lot of money. But he was a miser. He made the donkey work very hard, but gave him nothing to eat. He tied the donkey to a tree with a long rope so that the animal could wander around eating grass.

This was the only food that the donkey got during the day.

Soon the weather became hot and all the grass dried up. With no food, the donkey became thin and weak. As the days passed, it became difficult for him to carry the heavy load. So, he started walking slowly.

This irritated the washerman and he started beating the donkey to make him walk faster.

The washerman thought, "Without food, the donkey will die and I will have to do all the work myself again."

Suddenly, he remembered the lion's skin that he had picked up a few days ago.

He thought, "If I place the lion's skin on the donkey and let him loose in the nearby cornfield, he can eat to his heart's content. People would think he is a lion and not stop him. In fact, they would run away, scared that he would eat them."

So, the washerman let his donkey loose in the field at night. The donkey ate to his heart's content and returned home happily in the morning. This went on for many days.

The cornfield owner was disturbed that his crop was being destroyed.

When he went to the field to check, he saw an animal that looked like a lion. He got scared and ran away.

The owner then sent his guards to the field. Late at night, the guards saw a lion come there. They were surprised to see him eating corn.

The guards thought he was a strange creature and hatched a plan to trap him.

One of the guards wore a brown sack and stood in the corner of the field. When the donkey looked up, he mistook the brown sack for another donkey. And lo! He brayed loudly in pleasure.

Hearing him bray, the guards realized that it was a donkey and not a lion. They caught hold of the donkey in disguise and beat him to death. Thus, the miserly washerman lost his donkey and was forced to do all the work himself again.

Moral: Cheats are always caught.

The Old Lion and the Greedy Traveller

A flock of pigeons was flying high in the sky. After some time, the pigeons saw plenty of grains lying on the ground. They were tempted to fly down and eat them, but the pigeon king stopped them.

He said, "Do not be tempted by the sight of grains. Think wisely. Have you ever seen so many grains on the ground? This could be a trap laid by a hunter to catch us."

Then the pigeon king started narrating a story to show how greed could land one in trouble.

* * *

Once, there was an old lion who was unable to hunt. So he thought of a clever plan to trap a prey without much effort.

One day, he sat on the banks of the river with a tuft of soft, golden yellow straw tucked between his paws. He then called out, "Dear travellers, come here and take this gold bracelet from me."

Everyone was scared of the lion and did not dare to get close to him. They knew that if they went too close to the lion, he would eat them.

But a greedy traveller was tempted by the gold bracelet. He stopped and asked, "Where is the bracelet? Show it to me."

The lion flashed the tuft of straw in the sun and it looked like a bracelet. But the traveller was not convinced. "How can I believe him?" he thought.

The clever lion spoke innocently to the traveller and convinced him that he would not harm him.

He asked the traveller to take a dip in the river and then take the bracelet from him.

When the greedy traveller stepped into the river for a dip, he was stuck in the mud. The lion immediately pounced on him and ate him.

The pigeon king ended his story by saying, "One should think carefully before making any decision. Let us not act in a hurry."

But a young pigeon disagreed with the king. He said to the other pigeons, "If we keep thinking about our decisions all the time, then we will all stay hungry."

He also said, "I don't think there is any harm in eating the grains. Let us go."

The other pigeons agreed with him. They all flew down to eat the grains. Unfortunately, it was indeed a trap set by a hunter. All the pigeons were trapped in the hunter's net.

The young pigeon realized his mistake and apologized to the king. The king pigeon forgave him and suggested a solution to escape from the hunter's net. He said, "When I say the word 'fly', all of you must fly up together. You will be able to lift the net along with you. If we work together, then nothing can stop us."

So, the pigeons flew together, lifting the net with them towards the sky.

The hunter was shocked to see the pigeons flying away with his net. He had lost both his net and the pigeons.

The pigeon king took the pigeons to his friend the mouse king. He knew that the mouse king could release them by biting the net. The mouse king called all his mice. All of them bit the net and freed the pigeons.

The pigeons thanked the mouse king and his mice friends. The birds realized that they should always think before acting. They also learnt that if they were united, they could achieve anything.

Moral: Unity is strength.

Four Friends

Once, there were four friends—a mouse, a deer, a crow and a tortoise. They loved each other a lot and lived together near a lake in the forest.

One day, the tortoise felt very restless. So, he decided to explore new places.

He told his friends that he was going away. The mouse said, "Be careful. You are not strong, but you are intelligent. Use your intelligence in times of trouble. Before you go, let me tell you the story of a jackal and an elephant."

* * *

There lived a pack of jackals in a forest. The jackals were very hungry for a long time due to the harsh summer. They badly wanted food and longed to eat the plump elephant.

An old jackal came up with an idea to kill the elephant.

He said, "We cannot kill the elephant with our strength. He is more powerful than us. We must use our intelligence to trick him and then kill him."

The old jackal went to the elephant the next day. He spoke to the elephant with a lot of respect.

"As you are the strongest in the forest, all the animals want you to become their king," said the jackal.

The sly jackal then invited the elephant to follow him to a place where the animals were waiting to crown him.

The foolish elephant believed the jackal's cunning words.

He followed the jackal to a swamp and got stuck in the wet, sticky mud. He struggled to come out of the mud but could not. The exhausted elephant died and the jackals ate him to their heart's content.

* * *

The mouse ended his tale by advising the tortoise, "You should use your intelligence. Might alone will not help you always." However, the tortoise ignored his friend's advice. He bid farewell to his friends and left for a new place. Unfortunately, when he reached a river, the tortoise was caught by a hunter.

The hunter tied up the tortoise with a rope. In the meantime, the mouse, the deer and the crow were very worried about the tortoise.

Soon they saw the tortoise. The mouse thought of a plan to save him. He told the deer to lie on the ground and pretend to be dead.

Alas! I should have listened to my good friends' advice.

He then told the crow to act like he was pecking at the dead deer. This would convince the hunter that the deer was indeed dead and he would be tempted to leave the tortoise.

The mouse told the deer, "As soon as the hunter comes near you, get up and run. I will bite the rope and free the tortoise."

As the mouse had predicted, the hunter was happy to see the dead deer. He said, "Deer meat! I will take it home with me. I will earn more money from both the tortoise and the deer meat."

The hunter left the tortoise on the ground and went to pick up the deer. As soon as he got near the animal, the deer got up and ran away.

The dejected hunter thought, "He runs so fast! I can't match his speed. At least I have the tortoise."

But when the hunter went back, he saw that the tortoise too had vanished. He realized that he should have been content with the tortoise.

The hunter had lost both the animals due to his greed.

The four friends—the mouse, the deer, the tortoise and the crow—returned to the lake and lived happily ever after.

Moral: **Use your brain in times of trouble.**

The Crane and the Crab

Once upon a time, a peacock ruled over the birds of the forest. One day, the peacock king fought a battle with the birds of the neighbouring forest. He won the battle with the help of his faithful army. So, he decided to reward the birds who had helped him.

The peacock king said, "The crow helped me the most and I want to reward him well. I will give him the entire forest that we have won. The crow can send me all the valuables from the forest and I will live my life in luxury."

The minister bird discouraged the peacock king. He said, "My Lord, do not make a hasty decision. Please do not be greedy about the future. Greed can bring sorrow and even cost us our lives. Let me tell you a story about a crane who was very greedy."

The minister bird started narrating a story about a beautiful lake that was filled with many water animals.

* * *

As a large number of fish were available in the lake, the cranes came there to eat. They waited patiently for the fish to come to the surface. Then they swooped down to eat them.

The cranes were greedy and ate even after they were full.

Thus, the number of fish in the lake started to reduce. Also, the fish became more careful and stayed away from the surface of the water.

When the cranes were not able to find food anymore, they left the lake.

But an old and cunning crane stayed back. He thought of a plan to get his food.

The next morning, the old crane sat on the shore of the lake looking very sad. A crab who had been watching the crane asked, "Why do you look so sad? Why are you not looking for fish to eat?"

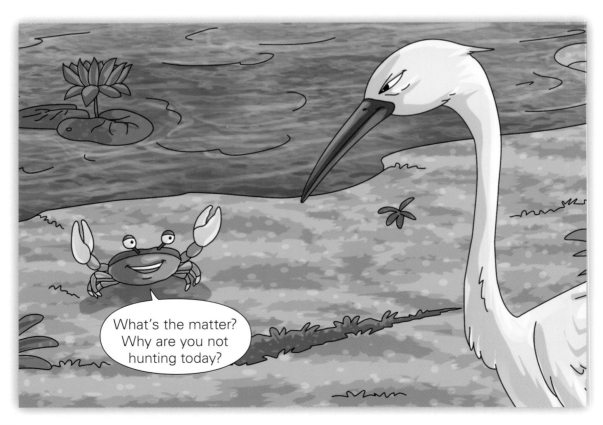

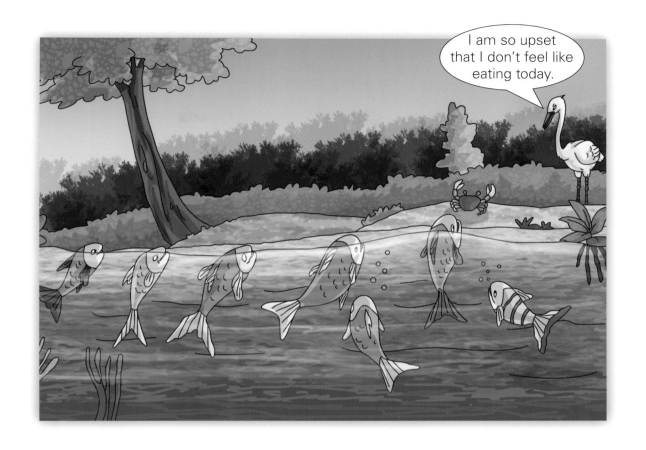

The crane replied, "While I was coming here, I overheard a few fishermen making plans to fish in this lake. They will take away all the remaining fish, and I will have no food. I also feel sorry for the fish and want to help them."

The news spread quickly to the fish in the pond. All of them became very sad.

The fish said to each other, "Although the crane is our enemy, he wants to help us in times of danger. Let us ask him how he plans to help us."

The crane said to the crab and the fish, "There is another big lake a little far away from here. I can take you all there, one by one, before the fishermen arrive. But you must trust me."

The fish and the crab agreed to this plan.

So, the cunning crane pretended to help the fish. He took them one by one in his beak, flew away to a lonely spot, and ate them. Soon he started looking fat.

One day, the crab said, "It is my turn today. Please take me to the lake."

The crane thought, "Today I will eat crab meat. It will be a different and tasty meal."

The crane took the crab to the lonely spot. The crab saw the bones of the fish there and immediately understood what the greedy crane had been up to.

The moment the crane put the crab down on the ground to eat it, the crab caught hold of the crane's neck with his claws and killed him.

* * *

The minister bird ended his story with the warning that the crane's greed had caused his death.

The peacock king realized his mistake. He did not give the crow the entire kingdom.

Instead, he thanked the crow and gave him precious gifts and some money. Then he ruled both the forests for a long time.

Moral: Greed leads to misery.

Meanings of Difficult Words

<u>The Curious Monkey</u>

stumbled	:	tripped; slipped and fell while walking or running
entangle	:	get caught in something in such a way that it is not easy to get out
wedge	:	a piece of wood or metal
poking	:	prodding or pushing someone or something with a finger or an object
crushed	:	compressed; flattened
curiosity	:	eagerness to know more about something

<u>The Birds and the Monkeys</u>

explore	:	travel to new places to learn something about them
farewell	:	goodbye
secure	:	safe from harm or danger

huddled	:	sat close to each other in order to stay warm
pleading	:	begging earnestly
misunderstood	:	understood the wrong way

The Donkey in a Lion's Skin

dawn	:	the start of morning when light appears in the sky
pile	:	a large number of things placed one on top of the other
prospered	:	grew; did well
miser	:	a person who saves all the money he earns and does not spend
hatched	:	planned something secretly, especially something bad

The Old Lion and the Greedy Traveller

tempted	:	attracted towards something
tuft	:	a lock of hair or grass

bracelet	:	a piece of jewellery worn around the wrist
pounced	:	jumped on something or someone
disagreed	:	opposed or argued due to a different view

Four Friends

restless	:	impatient and unable to stay still, because one is bored
swamp	:	an area of land that is flooded with water
predicted	:	foretold or guessed what would happen in the future
dejected	:	sad and disappointed
vanished	:	disappeared

The Crane and the Crab

luxury	:	something expensive and enjoyable, not necessarily something you need
discouraged	:	warned against; prevented
patiently	:	without complaining

swooped	:	moved quickly and suddenly through the air to attack or catch someone or something
precious	:	of great value; priceless